DiNo RiDERS

How to Track a Pterodactyl

Don't miss:

How to Tame a Triceratops

How to Rope a Giganotosaurus

How to Hog-Tie a T-Rex

How to Catch a Dino Thief

DINO RIDERS

How to Track a Pterodactyl

Will Dare

sourcebooks
jabberwocky

Published by Sourcebooks Jabberwocky, an imprint of Sourcebooks, Inc.
P.O. Box 4410, Naperville, Illinois 60567-4410
(630) 961-3900
Fax: (630) 961-2168
sourcebooks.com

Library of Congress Cataloging-in-Publication data is on file with the publisher.

Source of Production: Versa Press, East Peoria, Illinois, USA
Date of Production: July 2018
Run Number: 5012660

Printed and bound in the United States of America.
VP 10 9 8 7 6 5 4 3 2 1

With special thanks to Jonny Leighton.

CHAPTER 1

Josh Sanders lifted up his hat to wipe the sweat off his brow, then plonked it back on his head. The summer sun was hotter than a dinosaur's armpit, and there wasn't even a lick of wind to cool him down. The heat didn't bother Josh too much, though. Not now. He'd finally rounded up the last of the iguanodons on his family's ranch, and it was time to have some fun.

"Yee-haw!" Josh cried, grinning from ear to ear. "Let's go, lazybones!"

Josh kicked his heels, and his burly triceratops, Charge, sprang into action. The giant dino lifted his head into the air, howled into the sky, and kicked up a cloud of dust as they set off across the Sanders' ranch. Charge was as happy as Josh. All summer long, they'd been out on the dusty plains with his dad, herding stinky iguanodons. Now, they could do what they wanted, and Josh had a plan.

"Giddyap, boy!" Josh cried. "We've got places to be."

First, they were going to the annual Trihorn County Funfair—the biggest funfair in Trihorn and maybe even the whole of the

Dino-themed funfair attractions at the Trihorn County Fair

* **The Dino-Go-Round:**
  So much fun!

* **Haunted House:**
  Features the ghost of
  One-Legged Pete, the first
  Wild West pirate, and No-Head
  Hattie, who carries her
  head around in her arms.

* **Tin Can Alley:**
  Shoot the cans and
  win a stuffed dino!

Lost Plains. Then, they were going camping with Josh's best pals, Sam and Abi. Josh's dad had given Charge a ton of camping supplies to carry, while his mom had filled his saddlebags with as much food as he could manage. School was still a week away, and Josh was in the mood for adventure!

Charge galloped across the plains and toward town. Soon, Josh caught his first glimpse of the funfair, set up just on the edge of town.

"Whoa!" he cried. "Check it out, Charge."

A giant wooden roller coaster looped through the air. A Ferris wheel seemed to hang in the sky like a giant spider's web. All sorts of games and stalls were set up, already bustling with people. Everywhere Josh looked, dinosaurs of

4

different shapes and sizes were carrying fun seekers to Trihorn Settlement: gallimimuses, ankylosaurs, brontosaurs. As Josh and Charge got closer, he even had to duck down in his saddle as the spiky tail of a stegosaurus nearly knocked him clean off Charge.

"Hey, watch it!" he cried. The stegosaurus coach driver didn't even hear him; he just carried on his way. The dinosaur stopped at the entrance to the funfair, and about fifty passengers climbed down the stairs off its back. "Sheesh. Some people, eh, Charge?"

Suddenly, Josh heard familiar voices from behind him.

"What are you complaining about now, Dino Rider?"

"Yeah. We thought you could handle any dino, big or small."

Josh looked around and saw the familiar faces of his best friends, Sam and Abi, and their dinosaurs, Nickel and Fire. He broke into a wide grin. "Guys!" he cried. "You're here!"

"Of course we're here, pal," Abi said. "Have you seen this place?"

"Yeah," Sam nodded vigorously. "I've never seen so much candy in my life!"

It certainly was impressive. As they made their way into the fair together, Josh noticed loads of dino-themed goods for sale. There were huge plumes of cotton candy in the shape of T. rexes and licorice whips in the shape of a dino rider's lasso. The air was filled with the smell of toffee apples, and the crowds of people were slurping down Happy Ranch Cola like there was no tomorrow.

"What have you guys been up to?" Josh asked. Since he'd been working on the ranch, he hadn't had much time to see his friends over the summer. Soon, he realized he hadn't missed out on much.

"I trekked pretty much the whole length of the Lost Plains with my mom and dad, looking for purple turnips," Abi said.

"Huh? Purple turnips?" Josh asked.

"Yup. For the grocery store," she explained. "Apparently, they're the next big thing."

"Riiiiiiight," Josh said. "That sounds like fun?"

Abi pulled a face like she was chewing on a pickled wasp. "No," she said. "No, it was not."

"Hmm. How about you, Sam?" Josh asked hopefully.

Sam beamed with excitement. "Well," he began. "First, I researched the history of the Lost Plains. Then, I researched the geology of the Wandering Mountains' rock structure. There are just so many varieties of rock that—"

Before Josh fell asleep on the spot, he cut Sam off. "So basically," he said, "you did school-work. During summer vacation."

"Err…" Sam hesitated.

"I'll take that as a yes." Josh laughed. "But if we've all had kinda boring summers, that can only mean one thing."

"What's that?" Abi asked.

"It's definitely time for an adventu—
AARGHHH!" Josh jolted forward and clutched
his head. "Holy dino dung! What was that?"

Behind him, he heard a familiar, unwelcome
laugh. As he turned, he saw the mean face of
Amos Wilks leering at him. The bully's bulky
frame practically blocked out the sun. Arthur,
his weedy sidekick, skulked around too with a
nasty smirk stretched across his face.

"Oopsie," said Amos in a singsong voice. "I
didn't see you there."

"You should be more careful." Arthur
sniggered.

The children were right by the coconut shy,
where people throw hard, wooden balls at the

coconuts, hoping to win a big prize. Amos *just happened* to throw one that hit Josh—but nothing was a coincidence where Josh's nemesis was concerned.

"I ought to lasso you good and proper and tie you up for the T. rexes to snack on!" Josh started, but Abi and Sam held him back.

"Honestly, it was a mistake." Amos laughed out loud. "Watch this."

Amos juggled the balls in his hands and then chucked one right at the coconut shy. Somehow, even though the coconut stands were a couple of feet apart, he managed to knock two of them off. The stall owner was impressed and rummaged under the counter.

"Here you go, son." The old man beamed. "First prize!"

The old man handed over a bolo tie for Amos to wear around his neck. The long piece of cord that went around the neck was held together by a bright and shiny golden clasp embossed with the shape of a proud T. rex. It was one of the coolest bolo ties the kids had ever seen.

"Ah man," Josh moaned. He could barely conceal his jealousy.

Amos grinned his toothy grin. "Who's the hotshot now, eh?"

"Just ignore him," Abi said. "He's just showing off."

"Yeah," Sam chimed in. "Like always!"

Josh decided to take Abi's advice and just ignore Amos. It was always better that way. Anyway, he didn't have too much time to be annoyed about him, because something in the funfair crowd caught his eye. Suddenly, everyone seemed to be moving in one direction. A whispered bit of chatter became excited cries, and the whole fair jostled and jockeyed for position. Josh stopped a passerby who was hurriedly making her way toward a makeshift stage at the center of the fair.

"What's going on, miss?" he inquired.

"Why, young fella," she began. "It's the

official grand opening of the fair. And you'll never guess who they got to do the honors this year."

"Who?" Sam, Abi, and Josh cried in unison.

"None other than Terrordactyl Bill!"

CHAPTER 2

"T-Bill?" Josh asked. He couldn't believe it. T-Bill was his all-around hero and only the fastest, meanest, and bravest dino rider the Lost Plains had ever seen. T-Bill had outrun the fastest of T. rexes and wrestled giganotosauruses single-handed. Josh had met him once at the annual settlement race and always followed his exploits in the *Daily Diplodocus*, but he couldn't believe he'd be back in town opening their little old funfair.

"C'mon, guys. Quick!"

Josh, Sam, and Abi made their way through the crowds. Amos and Arthur rolled their eyes as if T-Bill was the lamest thing ever, but they still followed close behind. No one would want to miss the biggest hero in the Lost Plains, no matter how cool they thought they were.

Josh got as close as he could to the stage in the center of the funfair. Up high on the wooden platform stood his hero in the flesh. He had a big barrel chest and a mustache that had more bristles than tumbleweed rolling across a dusty plain. The clasp on his silver

bolo tie and the silver dino-tooth belt buckle around his waist shone out like precious gems, glinting in the sunlight.

"Wow!" Josh exclaimed. "Isn't he cool?"

"*Wowwww*," Amos mocked, putting on a babyish voice. "*Isn't he cooool?*"

"Shut up, you," Josh said, nudging Amos in the ribs. "You think he's as awesome as I do."

Amos just scowled back at Josh, but he couldn't resist a peek at T-Bill. Up on stage, the legend himself took a step forward and began to address the crowd.

"Ladies and fellas! Boys and girls! I welcome you to the annual Trihorn County Funfair!"

A cheer went up from the crowd, and everyone pressed closer.

"I hope you crazy Trihorners are all having a wild time!"

Another cheer went up, and people started chanting Bill's name.

"You guys really outdid yourselves this year."

The crowd went wild.

"It sure beats tusslin' with those bandits up by the Crocodile Cliffs," T-Bill continued.

A few murmurs went up from the crowd. No one knew what he was talking about.

The mayor, however, who was up on stage, knew exactly what Bill was up to. Talking about the Crocodile Cliffs was just a way for Bill to launch into a story. He was the best dino rider ever, but he did like to show off a bit. T-Bill told the crowd about his latest escapade, fending off bandits and crocodiles all at the same time, not forgetting to mention how much of a hero he was all the while.

"What a guy," Josh said.

"Yeah," Abi agreed. "And modest too."

T-Bill began to wrap up his story, explaining to the crowd how he escaped from a crocodile-infested swamp with only a teaspoon and a piece of string, when, suddenly, a piercing shriek went up in the crowd and T-Bill stopped mid-sentence.

Josh whipped his head around. He was about to tell whoever it was to be quiet. Didn't they know T-Bill was in the middle of a story? Or that he was in a life-and-death situation and somehow a piece of string and a teaspoon were going to get him out of it? But then, another scream went up from the crowd. Then another. And another…and that made Josh take note.

Josh looked up to where people where pointing. High in the skies, a dark shadow was forming. He wondered if it was a dark cloud, but no, it was something much more sinister than that.

"Uh-oh," said Sam. "I think I know what that is."

"Oh yeah?" Abi asked. "Please tell me it's something friendly. Or, you know, at worst a swarm of bees. Yeah…a swarm of bees would be just fine."

Sam gulped. "More like a swarm of *pterodactyls*!"

Right on cue, the black mass broke apart. The

pterodactyls broke formation and swooped down from the clouds. Ten pterodactyls dived down, leathery wings flapping urgently and scaly beaks snapping in the wind. The lead pterodactyl let out a cry that cut through the air like a knife.

Josh let out a huge bellow. *"RUN!"* he cried.

The crowd didn't need any encouragement. Hundreds of screaming people all made for the funfair gates where their dinosaurs were waiting. Shouts went up, and the whole town hummed with panic.

"Sam, watch out!" Josh cried.

A pterodactyl swooped down and snapped at Josh's friend. Just in time, Josh readied his lasso and whipped the hungry, flying dino on the beak.

"Yikes, that was close," Sam said. "We need to get out of here."

"No kidding, brainiac!" Abi cried.

Josh, Sam, and Abi sprinted back to their dinosaurs. Charge was tied up but ready for action. As soon as he saw Josh, he raised his three horns in the air like a soldier ready for battle.

"Where are we going?" Abi demanded. "Shelter?"

"I reckon so," Sam said. "If one of those things snaps at you, you're a goner!"

Josh hesitated. On one hand, Charge was clearly up for a fight. But on the other, they needed to get to safety. As he was thinking, a shout went up behind him, and suddenly, his mind was made up.

"Argh! Get off me, you big-beaked monster!" Amos cried.

"Argggghhh!" Arthur shouted, flapping his hands and running around in circles like he was trying to fly. "Get it off me. Get it off me!"

That's it, Josh thought. *They may be jerks, but they're not gonna get eaten on my watch.*

He yanked Charge free of his tie and jumped straight on. "Get to safety," he yelled at the others. "I've got dino riding to do!"

With a quick heel kick, Josh spurred Charge into action. He gripped his lasso tighter. Then, once he was in range, he snapped it forward, striking the ptero right on its leathery wing. It screeched a high-pitched wail and turned to face Josh.

"It's trying to eat me!" Amos shouted in alarm. "Either that or it's trying to get my bolo tie!"

"I think there's more important things going on than your stupid tie, Amos," Josh shouted back. "Let him have it!"

Josh ran at the ptero, making it flap its leathery wings and hover menacingly in the sky. He urged Amos and Arthur to jump on to Charge, which they did in an instant, but the pterodactyl dived in to attack once more…and this time, it brought a friend.

"Yargh!" Josh cried. "Get back, you ugly critters."

Josh, Amos, and Arthur were pinned down. The pteros were after them. Luckily, there was a hero nearby.

"T-Bill!" Josh cried as the burly wrangler came running toward them, lasso at the ready.

"I saw you were in a bit of a flap," T-Bill joked. With a whip in each hand, he snapped at the pteros. T-Bill managed to get them under some sort of control. Josh reckoned they were mesmerized by the power of the legend.

But despite T-Bill's efforts, Amos and Arthur kept screaming. The pteros that had been distracted by Bill started to take notice once more. They swooped at Amos, and this time, one of them snatched at his neck, coming away with his bolo tie. An inch further and Amos would have been dead as a doornail. He wailed in protest, more bothered about his tie than his life.

The shrieking of the pterodactyls made the others join in, and soon, nearly all of them were surrounding the children and T-Bill. Josh watched helplessly as T-Bill valiantly tried to fend them off. But it was no use. The pteros kept coming, lunging at him from all sides.

"Uh-oh," T-Bill shouted. "Run for it, kids!"

In an instant, the pteros surrounded him. With a shriek that pierced the air, they swooped down, snatched him up in their beaks, and carried him into the sky.

CHAPTER 3

J osh let out a wail of despair.

"*Nooo!*" he cried. But it was no use. T-Bill soared into the sky, carried by the screeching pterodactyls.

"My tie!" Amos wailed, reaching his hands out into the air for the shiny tie that was long gone.

Josh balled his fists in anger. "You and your stupid bolo tie!" he cried. "T-Bill just got abducted by pterodactyls!"

"But it was precious," Amos whined.

"And now it's g-g-gone!" Arthur added.

Josh was exasperated. T-Bill was gone too! But all Amos cared about was his stupid, shiny bolo tie.

Sam, Abi, and the crowds of people at the funfair slowly began to emerge from their hiding places. No one was sure what to do now that the rides had been stopped and the stalls pushed over in the crush to escape. Some of the old-timey ranchers and dino riders shook their heads in dismay.

"He was a fine chap, that T-Bill," said one.

"True enough," said another, stroking his long beard. "The Lost Plains won't see the likes of him any time soon."

Josh stared at them, wide-eyed in disbelief. "What are you talking about?" he asked. "Is no one going to do anything?"

"Too late, young man," one old-timer said. "The pteros have taken him."

Josh gritted his teeth. The greatest dino rider the Lost Plains had ever seen deserved better than that. He wasn't about to let T-Bill get eaten by a pack of hungry pterodactyls.

"We can't give up on T-Bill so easily," Josh said defiantly. "We are going to get him back!"

Sam and Abi looked on dubiously. The pteros were famously aggressive and terrifying creatures. Getting someone back from their clutches was almost unheard of. In fact, they wondered if anyone had even tried.

Then, an unlikely supporter stepped forward.

"I'll come," said Amos. "And Arthur will too!"

Josh looked shocked. Arthur did too. Poor Arthur was used to being told what to do by mean Amos, but he didn't look like he appreciated it this time one bit.

"But," Josh began, "you don't even like T-Bill."

"And s-since when do *we* want to go on a mission with this lot?" Arthur added.

"I know," said Amos. "But I want my bolo tie back!"

Josh groaned. He knew there would be a selfish explanation for Amos wanting to come. But he also knew that getting T-Bill back would be a challenge, and he reckoned that five people would be better than three.

Josh held out his hand and heartily shook Amos's. "That settles it then," Josh declared. "Abi, Sam, are you with me?"

Sam and Abi both nodded in unison. Even though they'd looked uncertain, Sam and Abi would never turn down an adventure.

"We're with you," they said.

With four out of five signed up, Arthur didn't want to be left out. He quickly nodded his head in agreement.

Josh grinned from ear to ear. "In that case, summer isn't over quite yet, pals. We have an adventure to go on!"

Abi led the way as the group rode out of Trihorn Settlement and onto the dusty, cactus-littered plains surrounding it. Small lizards skittered about beneath their feet, and flies buzzed around their heads. The sun was sinking lower in the sky, but there was still time to make some progress before nightfall.

"Where we headed, Abi?" Josh asked.

"North," she said. "Toward the Wandering Mountains. My folks and me came up this way earlier this summer. They say that the pteros live way up high in the hills."

"That's right," Sam jumped in. "I read about them. There's a whole colony of them up on one of the higher peaks."

Arthur jumped into the conversation from atop his gallimimus, Cobalt. "B-but wouldn't that m-mean," he stammered, "that we'd have to go over Rocktooth Ridge?"

"What's that?" Amos snapped. "And what does it matter? We need to get my bolo tie back!"

Sam frowned a little and tugged at his shirt collar. "Well," he began. "It's a narrow path at the top of one of the Wandering Mountains. It's quite high up and pretty treacherous."

"And why do they call it Rocktooth?" Amos barked.

"Oh, you know," Sam said. "Because on either side of it, there's a hundred-foot drop. And if you fell, you'd land on one of hundreds of spiky rocky outcrops that kinda look like T. rex teeth and, well, would definitely kill you quicker than a quick draw at high noon."

The others went silent. Tumbleweed skittered across the road in front.

"And remind me why we're doing this," Abi said.

"For T-Bill!" Josh said seriously. "And apparently for Amos's bolo tie. But it's fine. No one's going to fall off. I promise."

Secretly, Josh was a little bit worried, but he didn't want to show it. They were going on an adventure, and they were going to save T-Bill. That was final. Whatever came their way, they'd just have to deal with it.

The dinosaurs trooped miles out of town, speedily carrying them in the direction of the Wandering Mountains. As they got nearer to the mountains, the foothills became more difficult. Josh sensed Charge working a bit harder as the ground got steeper. But it wasn't just that. The ground was covered in loose pebbles and stones. Every time Charge and the other dinos tried to get a grip, the gravel surface would slip away from under them.

"Come on, Charge!" he cried.

The others also urged their dinos on. Sam and Abi's gallimimuses, Nickel and Fire, tried to skip lightly across the ground but failed. Amos's ankylosaurus, Clubber, and Arthur's gallimimus, Cobalt, also struggled. They were both so heavy that the ground seemed to slip away right from under them.

Soon, Amos got frustrated. "Blast it!" he shouted. "Going slowly is no use. If we run up this slope, then we can make it to the plateau up there." He pointed up ahead of him to where the foothills seemed to level out before going upward once more toward the rock peaks.

"Wait, no!" Sam cried. "We have to tread carefully."

But it was too late. Amos spurred Clubber and went shooting off up the rocky foothill. At first, he seemed fine. The heavy ankylosaurus clambered up the scree slope like a bullet eagerly escaping a gun. But then, a low cry rang out as Clubber seemed to lose his footing. In a flash, the dinosaur had fallen on its scaly backside, Amos clinging on for all he was worth as they barreled down the hill, back toward the other riders.

"Uh-oh!" Josh cried quickly. *"Incoming!"*

CHAPTER 4

uick!" shouted Abi. "Do something!"

But there was nothing Josh could do. Clubber barreled toward them like an out-of-control bowling pin.

"Yargh!" they all yelled together.

Clubber barged into Cobalt, who slammed into Fire, who crashed into Nickel, who made a beeline straight for Charge. Josh gripped the reins tight until his knuckles were white as he

tried to think of an escape plan, but it turns out that when four dinosaurs come tumbling toward someone, there's not much they can do.

With an almighty crash, all five dinos slid down the foothill and ended up in a heap on the valley floor. The five riders flew through the air and ended up in their own tangled heap of arms and legs. Josh heaved himself up from the crush and noticed his face was about an inch away from a giant pile of dino dung.

"Urgh," he cried, heaving himself up. "Nice one, Amos. Now look what you've done."

Amos sheepishly rubbed his head. "That hill is tougher to climb than it looks!"

"Too right," said Josh. "You know what this means? We're going to have to scale the hill on foot. There's no way the dinos are going to get up there."

The others reluctantly agreed. They'd have to leave the dinos down below. The gallimimuses had untangled themselves and were sitting on the ground looking miserable. Even Charge looked a little downcast. Clubber, the brutish ankylosaur, scuffed the ground. It seemed like the dinosaurs agreed too.

As the sun had already begun to dip lower over the mountains, the group decided that there was nothing left to do but to turn in for the night. Together, they found a sheltered spot to tie the dinos up, and Josh fed them all one of the pies his mom had made. The kids had some too, making funny faces as they tried to guess what weird ingredients Josh's mom had put in this time. Then, they pitched the tent in the shadow of a huge cactus that was three or four times the height of Josh. They figured they could tap the plant for water and that it might provide a bit of shade when the sun rose.

Luckily, Josh had been prepared for camping that day. Unluckily, he hadn't expected Amos and Arthur to be involved. Before he knew it, they were all arguing as they struggled to pitch the tent.

"Put the peg in this way, pea brain," Amos barked. "Not *that* way!"

Josh grumbled. It wasn't as if he'd never put up a tent before. He decided to leave the

Lost Plains Campfires 101

How to pitch a tent:
-Step 1:
Read instructions.

-Step 2:
Get angry at instructions.

-Step 3:
Just do it the best you can.

Food:
-Pies from Mom
-Sam's pillowcase stuffed
 full of marshmallows
-Ye Olde Timey Sarsaparilla
 from Abi's Grocery Store

Songs:
-"We're All Going on a Dino Hunt!"
-"Heads, Shoulders, Knees, and Lassos"

How to ward dinos off your tent:
-Trip wire around your
 tent with bells on
-Build a scare-dino (a bit like
 a scarecrow but much
 more fearsome)

others to it and started building a campfire. He collected some wood for kindling and dug a pit with a small spade he carried in Charge's saddlebag. Charge helped widen the hole with his giant dino claws. Just as the sky went from deep blue and purple to silky black, the fire roared into life. With the tent finally up and the first stars beginning to twinkle, Josh felt like he was in his element.

"How's this for a summer adventure?" he said as they settled in around the campfire.

Sam tried to say something in agreement, but he'd stuffed so many marshmallows in his mouth, it came out as a muffled huff of air.

"Errmm, you know you're supposed to toast those, right?" Abi offered.

"Oh yeah." Sam laughed, finally swallowing the sweet treats. "But who has time for that?"

He offered them around, and they each found their own stick to roast them on. Soon, the air smelled of sticky-sweet deliciousness. However, Amos was quick to burst their bubble.

"You know what they say about these plains, don't you?" he began.

Abi sighed. "No, what? They're haunted by the ghosts of cactuses past?"

Amos snorted. "No, you dingus. I mean really. They say that this is where the egg rustlers come. This is the path they take to the pterodactyl hideout. And they're ruthless with anyone they find trespassing on their territory. They tie 'em up by their legs and hang them upside down to roast in the midday sun!"

Suddenly, the plains felt empty and scary. The hooting of an owl sent a shiver down Josh's spine. He'd heard stories about egg rustlers—people daring to scale the heights of the Rocktooth Ridge just to grab a few ptero

eggs. He could never understand why they did it. Josh and his friends were only going because they had a hero to rescue. Why would anyone want pterodactyl eggs?

"Erm, guys," Amos said. "Where's Arthur?"

The others looked around. Arthur had suddenly disappeared. Josh, Sam, and Abi looked at each other in alarm.

"But he was here a minute ago!" Abi cried.

"W-what if one of the egg rustlers got him?" Sam replied.

Josh stood up. He was going to have to go into the darkness to find him. But just as he was about to step out of the campfire's light, he heard a rustling sound. Then he felt a hand on his shoulder…

"*Boo!*"

"Yargh!" Josh yelled, readying his lasso. But before he could, Amos and Arthur were doubled over, laughing.

"Ha ha ha, loser," Amos said. "We got you good!"

"Yeah," Arthur added. "R-r-real good!"

Josh frowned. If there really were rustlers out on these plains, Amos and Arthur would totally have alerted them by now. Josh gave up trying to stop them whooping and hollering and decided he'd had enough of camping for one night. He, Sam, and Abi were going to bed.

"Enjoy sleeping outside," he called to Arthur and Amos.

"I don't think so, partner," Amos called.

All of a sudden, there was a mad rush to the tent. All five of them struggled and elbowed and battered their way into the three-person tent. When they were all finally in there, it was practically bursting at the seams. Josh managed to zip closed the front door, then snuggled down under one of the blankets. Unfortunately for Josh, he soon began to get a whiff of something nasty—a bit like cheese mixed with one of Charge's legendary burps.

"Eww, what is that?" he said, gasping for air.

"Oh, just my feet," Amos declared proudly. "G'night, dweebs. Don't let the egg rustlers bite!"

Josh turned away, making sure his face wasn't right in Amos's stinky feet. He wasn't sure what was worse: the prospect of sleeping next to smelly Amos all night or egg rustlers roaming the plains.

Outside, he heard the dinosaurs shuffling and then gently snoring. In the distance, animal noises echoed through the quiet. He took a deep breath, closed his eyes as tight as possible, and tried his hardest to fall asleep.

It's gonna be a long night, he thought as he drifted into slumber.

CHAPTER 5

Josh woke with a cough and a splutter. Somehow in the night, he'd managed to get even closer to Amos's stinky feet.

Blurgh, he thought. *Time to get out of here.*

He quickly unzipped the tent door and stepped out into the bright morning, gulping in the fresh air. The Lost Plains weren't half as creepy in the sunshine. Instead, the Wandering Mountains rose high into the air like a tempting challenge. He just hoped that T-Bill could fight off those pteros long enough to stay alive and get himself rescued.

Josh made his way over to Charge and the other dinos. He was about to fetch them some fresh grass and water when he stopped dead in his tracks. Someone had already done it. Charge and the others were happily munching on a fresh mound of grass.

"What the—" he began. But before he had time to answer his own question, a wild-haired woman stepped out from behind Charge.

"Well, howdy there, trekker!" she began. "'Bout time you young lazybones got up!"

Josh frowned. He had no idea who this woman was. She stood before him, out of nowhere, like a one-woman mountain. Her gray hair was curled up high on her head like a storm cloud, and she was swathed in strange material that was part rough fabric, part dino skin. She had a dino horn and a dagger attached to a sling on her waist. It was a Trihorn Toothpick if Josh wasn't mistaken—sharp and deadly as they come. She looked as though she had stepped out of the landscape itself.

"Uh, who are you?" he mumbled.

"Rona Rawfoot," she said and smiled. "Or Ramblin' Rona as they call me. I live out here on the plains. There's nothing like the fresh air and the sweet smell of dinos in the mornin', I say! I hope you don't mind, but I gave your steeds over there some water and something to eat."

By now, Sam, Abi, Amos, and Arthur had woken up and wandered over. Rona introduced herself. Josh supposed it was OK that she'd fed the dinos. But it was a bit unusual.

"They call me a mountain woman," Rona explained. "I live out here on my own, making my way on what I can forage from the land. I take care of the land, and the land takes care of me."

"Cooool," said Sam. "I always wanted to meet a proper mountain woman!"

"Well, now you have, kiddo," she said, laughing heartily. But when she'd finished, her expression changed. She narrowed her eyes slightly and looked around at the gaggle of kids at her feet. "But what are *you* doing out here? That's the question."

Rona Rawfoot Profile

Dino horn for sounding alarms

Dino skin waistcoat

Trihorn Toothpick: a dagger for fending off angry dinosaurs

Josh was about to reply when Arthur piped up instead. "We're going up to R-r-rocktooth Ridge!" he blurted.

Josh nudged him in the ribs. For some reason, he didn't want Rona to know that. A funny thought was flitting across his mind. She played the part of mountain woman well, but what if she was an egg rustler? That dagger she was carrying was plenty sharp enough, that was for sure. Wouldn't that be just what a rustler used?

Rona Rawfoot looked at the children and raised an eyebrow. "Oh, I see," she said slowly. "Well, funnily enough, I was going that way too. How about we go together? It might be easier that way."

Josh shook his head quickly but not quickly enough.

"Sure!" Abi cried. "We can't get up these slopes without help!"

"Well then, that's settled," Rona said. "As soon as you happy campers have cooked up some breakfast, we'll get going!"

Josh frowned. What if they led her right to the pterodactyls' hideout? She'd been quick to join them when she heard about Rocktooth Ridge. But then he had a thought. If Rona was determined to scale Rocktooth Ridge with them, then at least he would be able to keep an eye on her. If she was a no-good egg rustler, he might be able to do something about it. Maybe when they rescued T-Bill, he'd be able to help too.

Quickly as they could, they whipped up some breakfast with the remains of their food, packed up their tent equipment, and put out the campfire. Everything they couldn't carry they left with the dinos for safekeeping. Josh gently told Charge that they'd be right back, but the triceratops still whimpered as they left.

The trek was tough but not as tough as when they'd been on their dinos. Rona Rawfoot did seem to know the way at least. They were soon making great progress, zigzagging their way up the scree slope instead of charging on ahead as before. Quickly, the loose scree gave way to hard rock, and all six of them had to use both arms and legs to scramble up the mountain-side. Josh began to feel giddy as the ground disappeared below him. A wisp of cloud floated right in front of him, and he could see they were getting higher.

After a morning's climb, fingers, legs, and arms aching, they eventually made it up to a flat piece of rock, about halfway up the mountain. Rona stretched out her arms and beckoned the children to take a look.

"Well," she said. "The Lost Plains ain't too bad to look at, are they? Certainly better than a sad dino on a wet day!"

"That's for sure!" Sam said. "I've always wanted to see the Lost Plains from up here!"

Josh remained suspicious, but Rona was right about the Lost Plains. They stretched before them like a huge tapestry, with ranches and settlements dotted about all over. From up there, he could see the Cold Fear Forest, the Scratchclaw Swamps, and the Loneheart Lakes, all at the same time.

However, there was still a lot more ground to cover. The group turned away from the amazing view and carried on toward their destination. Rona led them up a rocky path to another mountain ledge, and that's when they saw it: the famous Rocktooth Ridge.

"Whoa!" Josh gasped as pebbles and rocks tumbled down the steep fall below him. Right on cue, the wind began to rise and the air chilled, and all six trekkers found themselves shrouded in clouds. The ridge went from one side of the mountain to another, but it had no rock wall to hold on to. Instead, it was like a pirate's plank a hundred feet above spiny needles of rock and ice.

"That's a bit, erm, terrifying," Sam said.

"We eat fear for breakfast!" Josh said, puffing out his chest.

"Actually, we ate the leftovers of last night's dinner for breakfast—" Sam began.

"I didn't mean *literally*," Josh said. "Anyway, if I'm right, on the other side of this ridge, we'll find—"

"Pterodactyls," Rona said. "And plenty of them!"

Josh eyed her suspiciously—what would Rona want with pteros?—but it was too late to back down now. They were at the ridge, T-Bill needed rescuing, and there was no time to lose.

The group slowly edged over the perilous mountain pass. The whipping wind made the walk more treacherous, and Josh urged the others to hunker down. The closer they were to the rocky ground, the easier it would be to keep their balance. Josh peered below. The razor-sharp shards of rock were making him feel dizzy. He hoped that as long as he kept his head up and eyes forward, he would be OK.

Out in front, Amos and Arthur had crossed successfully. Rona and Abi were next, and Josh and Sam brought up the rear. Just as they passed the halfway mark, Josh heard a cry go up from behind him.

Sam? he thought.

Josh turned around on the narrow ledge as

quickly as he could, desperately trying to keep his balance. But poor Sam was even more unsteady on his feet. He'd slipped on the wet rock, and he was struggling to steady himself.

"Josh—" he cried as he lost his footing and his arms did windmills in the air.

Sam was about to fall off Rocktooth Ridge!

CHAPTER
6

Josh had to act fast. He gripped his lasso tight and whipped it out in front of him. "Grab on, Sam," he yelled.

The lasso snapped forward, and Sam held out a hand, grabbing it just in time. Josh lurched forward right to the edge of the ridge as Sam dropped helplessly below. A hundred feet beneath him, sharp rock glistened in the early morning sun, ready to snap up another victim.

"Argh!" Sam screamed. "Pull me up! Pull me up!"

"I'm trying!" said Josh, straining to hold the lasso. "Quick, guys, help!"

Abi, Arthur, Amos, and Rona all edged back along the ridge and grabbed onto the rope.

"OK, everyone, on the count of three," Abi began. "One…two…three!"

Together, all five of them yanked on the lasso. Sam slowly rose up the mountainside and clambered back onto the ridge, panting and heaving. He clambered to his feet, and the six of them dashed across the ridge, making it safely to the other side.

"Man, oh man!" Sam said as they huddled together. "That was close!"

"You gave us a scare," said Josh, bundling up his lasso and safely fastening it in his holster.

"Yeah. You know," Abi teased, "maybe you should cut down on the marshmallows, pal.

That was like hauling a sack of potatoes back at the grocery store."

"Hey," Sam said with a pout. "You weren't complaining when there were marshmallows toasting over a nice campfire!"

Even Amos and Arthur could agree with that.

"Anyway, guys, c'mon," said Sam. "We can't stick around here dangling off terrifying ridges all day. We've got T-Bill to rescue, remember?"

Rona gasped. "You what? T-Bill?"

"Yeah," Sam said. "That's why we're here. T-Bill got captured by a whole bunch of pterodactyls. They flew him up this mountain, and we're here to rescue him."

Josh was worried. If Rona knew that they were rescuing T-Bill, the most famous, law-abiding citizen in the Lost Plains, she might go back down the mountain and leave them stranded.

For a moment, Rona looked concerned. Then, a wide smile broke out on her face, and she did a huge belly laugh, until her body was bopping up and down like a rodeo clown. "T-Bill? Captured by pteros?" She laughed. "Well, I never. I got you kids all wrong."

"Huh?" Sam began. "What are you talking about?"

"Old T-Bill got himself into a scrape, and you're out here looking for him?" She laughed. "And here's silly old me thinking you young whippersnappers were egg rustlin'!"

Josh reeled back. Abi's and Sam's mouths

hung open in surprise. Ever Arthur and Amos seemed confused.

"Egg rustlers?" Josh asked. "We would never do something like that! We're here on a rescue mission! I thought *you* were the egg rustler."

At this, Rona Rawfoot let out an even bigger belly laugh. The belt around her waist jangled as the dino horn and the Trihorn Toothpick knocked together. "Look here, son," she began. "I'm the one fighting the darned egg rustlers! They sneak up here and disturb the pterodactyls' nests, stealing eggs so they can raise the pterodactyls as their own and teach them how to be criminals."

"But how come they don't get eaten?" Sam asked.

"Silly thing!" Rona said. "Pteros don't eat us folks. They eat smaller critters, bless them. They'd never get a big ol' human in their mouths."

"So then why do they attack us?" Josh asked.

Rona was about to reply, but her face suddenly dropped. She'd seen something behind Sam, something the kids were not going to like.

"Well, because they're mischievous critters that like a scrap, son," she said. "And it looks like we got a mighty fine specimen coming our way right about now!"

Josh heard the familiar screeching cry of a pterodactyl. He whipped his head up and saw it, hanging in the sky, beating its ferocious wings, sending a cloud of dust from the mountainside hurtling in his direction. Josh rubbed his eyes and blinked, but the dust cloud was blinding him.

"I have a fair idea where T-Bill will be," said Rona. "But we gotta make a break for it, folks. This one's angry. Run!"

All six continued up the mountain as best they could, but the angry ptero pecked at them at every turn. Josh realized that they must be getting close to wherever T-Bill was being kept. Why else would the ptero be so angry?

He let fly with his lasso a couple of times, long enough for them to take shelter behind a giant rock. Rona unsheathed her Trihorn Toothpick and waved it about in front of the ptero. It didn't seem fazed at all by the glinting blade. In fact, it seemed to rather like it. However, as the angry ptero continued its attack, the ground above them started rumbling.

"Oh, for the love of the Lost Plains," Arthur started. "What is that?"

"Shut it, dweeb," said Amos. "It's a rockfall! All the noise and commotion is bringing this mountain down around us."

Amos was right. Dust and pebbles were flying down the mountain at an alarming rate. Soon, they'd be completely covered, and they'd be swept off the mountain.

"C'mon fellers...and little lady!" Rona called. "This way. We ain't goin' any farther up this mountain. We're going *through*."

Josh wondered what Rona meant, but he was

soon to find out. The group followed Rona as best they could, rockfall on one hand, giant, angry pterodactyl on the other. They skipped over the lighter rocks, and suddenly, Josh saw it: a thin gap in the mountainside. They hauled themselves and each other through into what looked to be a mountain tunnel, Rona leading the way. Once they were inside, the ptero screeched furiously at them, but it couldn't follow them in thanks to the narrow tunnel walls.

"We should be safe in here for a while," Sam said.

"Don't bet on it," Abi said. "Listen!"

There was an almighty bang, like a T. rex roar mixed with a thunderbolt. It might have been the screeching or the commotion, but a giant

cloud of pebbles and rocks was flying down the mountainside outside.

Arthur and Amos clung together like a couple of scared baby dinos. Sam, Abi, and Josh pressed themselves against the tunnel walls. Rona was about to urge them onward when Josh let out a cry.

"Rockfall!"

CHAPTER 7

As hundreds of rocks tumbled down the mountain outside, dust and stones blew into the mountain tunnel. The world seemed to turn gray. Josh pressed himself up against the rock face as best he could to shield himself from the blast.

"Hang tight, guys!" he cried.

Dust and tiny stones seemed to flood the

tunnel. If they'd been out on the mountain ledge, they would certainly have been doomed.

Finally, after what felt like a lifetime, the rumbling stopped.

"I think it's over!" Josh said.

Sure enough, the waterfall of rocks and stones had stopped tumbling down, and their view cleared, like sunshine after a heavy rainfall. Josh noticed that all five of them were gray with soot and dirt, but apart from a few scrapes and scratches, they seemed to be OK.

Wait, he said to himself. *Five?*

"Where's Rona?" Abi asked. "She was in here a minute ago."

"She was just ahead of me, I'm sure," Sam said. He edged farther through the mountain tunnel. "I can barely see a thing, just a wall of rock. Oh wait."

"What is it?" Amos demanded, barreling forward.

"Oh yeah, just more rock. Sorry."

Amos sighed in frustration. "Rona was the only one of us who knew where to go. How on the Lost Plains am I ever going to get my bolo tie back now?"

"Yeah," Arthur agreed. "That's precious, you know."

Abi rolled her eyes and puffed out her cheeks. "You know we are here for another reason too, not just your stupid bolo tie."

But suddenly, Josh put his finger to his lips. "Quit it, Abi. I hear something!"

Abi looked annoyed, but Josh wouldn't shush her for no good reason. He cocked his head to the right like he was trying to catch something on the wind. "Is that a horn?"

The other children all strained to listen, and sure enough, they could hear a high, *toot-toot* noise and the hearty voice of Rona Rawfoot echoing from deep inside the mountain.

"This way!" Josh cried. "She must have ventured farther through. Let's go."

Josh led the others toward the sound. They squeezed through the narrow, dark tunnel, delving deeper into the mountain. Josh made light work of the rocks, skipping over them with newfound hope. Soon, he saw a narrow beam of light, and the group found themselves approaching an opening on the other side of the mountain.

"It's coming from out here," Josh said as another *toot-toot* sound pierced the sky. "Listen."

Quickly, the kids squeezed their way through the crack in the mountainside. Arthur almost got stuck, and Amos had to push him through like a mouse through the floorboards, but he made it. Josh clambered up the remaining few rocks, and suddenly, he could make out Rona and a familiar figure.

"T-Bill!" he cried. "You're alive!"

Josh, Sam, Abi, Amos, and Arthur all looked at each other in amazement. They'd found T-Bill!

"Well, of course I am, scamp," T-Bill said, his mustache twitching. "But no thanks to those pesky pterodactyls. And to think I call myself a dino rider."

"Pah." Rona laughed and brushed herself down. She'd gotten caught in the rockfall but made it to the other side of the mountain and found T-Bill at the same time. "It could happen to anyone."

"They sure made a mess of my leg," he said, pointing down to his foot, which looked a bit bruised and bashed up. "That's why I couldn't make it down."

"That and you're getting old," Rona said with a laugh.

Josh felt like he was missing out on

something. Rona and Bill were chatting as if they were old pals.

"Do you two know each other?" Josh wondered aloud.

"Know each other?" Rona gawped. "Well, of course! This old-timer and me go way back. He's why I'm out here on the plains in the first place."

T-Bill had a twinkle in his eye. "And she came to rescue me one more time, eh? Oh, and you young 'uns of course." T-Bill gestured around at the kids, who had gathered on the mountain-top. "Which I mighty appreciate, by the by."

"It's an honor!" Josh said heartily. "But I don't get it. How comes the pteros left you unharmed? Did you fight 'em off? Were they saving you for later?"

Rona Rawfoot let out a huge guffaw. "A ptero could never swallow him up—look at the size of him. Besides, look around, kiddo." She gestured to the high plain where T-Bill was stranded. The place was covered in all manner of shiny trinkets, bullets, metal…anything and everything that had a reflection.

"Pteros are only interested in shiny things, like T-Bill's buckle over there and that bolo tie I see."

"Bolo tie!" Arthur gasped. He rushed over to where it lay, scooped it up, and cradled it like a baby.

Suddenly, Josh understood. "So that's it!" he cried. "The pterodactyls are attracted to shiny things. That's why they were attacking people at the fair. That's why they hadn't eaten Bill up."

"And that's why you get egg rustlers, you see," Rona continued. "Thieves steal the eggs, raise the pteros as their own, then get them to steal all sorts of shiny things. But mostly cold, hard coins! That's what I've been out here all these years trying to stop. I know they can be a bit mean, the old pteros, but they don't deserve to have their eggs stolen. And they don't gotta be on the side of criminals. Am I right, Bill?"

"You sure are, Rona." Bill nodded. "But I could've done without one of those critters chewing on my leg!"

Josh couldn't argue with that. He was just

Pterodactyl Profile

Leathery wings for super-fast flight

Mean, squinty eyes

Long, sharp, stabby beak

Claws that can rip the badges off a sheriff's chest

happy that he'd managed to find his hero in one piece. Not bad for a day's work, he reckoned.

"But how are we gonna get you back down?" Abi cried. The wind at the top of the mountain was whirling around, loud and strong.

"Yeah," said Sam. "I mean, maybe we could carry you, but the path is kinda slippery. We had a bit of a rockfall incident. I don't think we'll even make it out the other side of the tunnel we just came through."

T-Bill stroked his mustache and pondered for a minute. But before he could come up with an answer, Arthur mumbled something.

"What's that, man?" Josh asked.

"I s-said," Arthur began, "that we've got

other things to worry about before we get off this mountain."

He pointed up at the sky, and Josh's stomach sank. There, freewheeling and careening through the skies, were the familiar shapes of the pterodactyls. The lead ptero let out a cry, high and shrill enough to shock the eardrums.

"Uh oh," he said. "The pterodactyls are back!"

CHAPTER 8

Josh readied his lasso. Sam and Abi stood behind him. If the pterodactyls attacked, they'd be ready to defend T-Bill, who struggled to get to his feet, but his mangled foot stopped him from springing into action. Amos and Arthur cowered in the corner as the pterodactyls drew closer. Rona Rawfoot looked on, defiant.

"Get behind me," Josh cried. "I'll try to fend them off."

Quickly, the winged monsters swooped down. They didn't appreciate that their treasure trove of goodies had been disturbed, and they weren't going to let the intruders go without a fight. They landed on the top of the mountain and surrounded everyone, flapping their wings.

"Erm, I hope you have a plan," said Abi. "Because I'm kind of out of ideas."

"Yeah," agreed Sam. "Maybe they like marsh-mallows? If I had any left…"

"They don't like marshmallows, but maybe we can fend them off with my lasso," Josh said. He cracked the rope against the ground, making the pteros flinch backward for a moment.

"That's enough!" said a voice from behind them. Rona Rawfoot took charge and moved ahead of the children. "They don't like violence, and they don't like no lassos. But we do know something that they like, don't we?"

Rona delved into one of her many pockets. Josh saw her bring out something shiny and round. The pteros immediately took notice, cawing and cooing like excited birds. Rona

threw the bottle cap on the ground, then another, and then another. The pteros slowly walked forward. They wanted the *new* shiny treasure.

"That's it, my lovelies," Rona said. "Come and get 'em!"

The pteros moved forward and delicately picked up the bottle caps. One by one, they transferred them to their lair. Josh couldn't believe what he was seeing. The pteros weren't interested in the children anymore at all. In fact, they seemed to even be quite friendly with them.

"You too, Amos," Rona said.

"Awww, really?" Amos cried. But he didn't see how he had a choice. He gently put down his beloved bolo tie as an offering to one of the pteros.

"Whoa!" said Josh. "How did you manage that?"

Rona beamed with pride. "See, you just have to be nice to them sometimes. I know it's hard when they're snapping at you, but they're friendly enough creatures, really."

Josh got so close to one of the pteros, he could stroke its leathery neck. Sam and Abi did too, getting a close-up look at the orangy-green pterodactyls. Amos and Arthur regained their courage, and T-Bill approached them too.

"Well, I never," he said. "I'm more used to wranglin' these critters than taming 'em."

"They ain't tame, Bill. They can be very

dangerous when they're angry," said Rona. "But if you catch 'em just right and treat them with a bit of respect, there's no need to fear 'em. Watch this."

Rona sidled up to a pterodactyl and gently stroked its neck. The dinosaur cooed like a friendly bird. Rona gave it another bottle cap that it quickly squirreled away in the corner of its mountain cave. Then, Rona did something Josh couldn't believe. She hopped right on the back of the ptero, like it was a regular old gallimimus or stegosaurus.

"Cool!" he gasped.

"Yup," she agreed. "Not bad for an old mountain wanderer, eh? And you know, it really is the quickest way down the mountain."

"You gotta be kidding me," Abi said.

"I certainly am not." Rona grinned. "Find yourself a partner and hop on!"

Josh, T-Bill, and the others sidled up to their own pteros. Josh couldn't believe it, but sure enough, one of the pteros let him jump on its back. Only moments ago, he'd been sure it was about to snap his head off, but now they were practically best friends.

As they all got in position, Rona gave her mark. "Are you ready?" she cried. The others nodded. Rona spurred her ptero, and it took off into the air. Josh did the same and soon found himself lifted high into the sky. He hung on as best he could as the ptero soared. He looked across at the others. Abi clung on

with one hand and lifted her hat into the air with the other. Sam's eyes were wide with joy. Even grumpy old Amos and Arthur seemed to be enjoying themselves. T-Bill looked as if he couldn't believe what he was doing.

"Yee-haw!" Josh cried as the Wandering Mountains disappeared below him. The Lost Plains looked beautiful from up high.

Quickly, Rona wheeled around to the left, and the other pteros followed. Josh spotted a group of dinosaurs down by a stream. He could see that it was Charge, Nickel, Fire, Clubber, and Cobalt. The pterodactyls glided safely to the ground and dropped off their passengers. Charge raised a horn in greeting to Josh but looked wary of the pteros.

"Charge!" Josh cried. Josh ran over and gave him a mighty pat on his flank. "I missed you, buddy!"

As soon as the pteros were free of their passengers, they took off and were soon soaring back into the sky. Josh and his friends waved good-bye. They'd managed to rescue T-Bill *and* fly a flock of pterodactyls all in one day. *Pretty impressive stuff*, Josh thought.

"So how about you give this old-timer a ride back to Trihorn?" T-Bill asked. "I could use something for this old foot of mine."

"Seriously?" Josh asked. "On Charge? I'd love to!"

"Well, all right then," said T-Bill. "Let's get going!"

T-Bill gave Rona a hug, and the others waved as she set off. She wasn't planning on coming back to Trihorn any time soon. Apparently, that "city" malarkey wasn't really for her, despite Trihorn being pretty small. But Josh understood—she was a mountain woman through and through.

"Just so long as you keep a look out for any rustlers out your way. If you find any, tell them Rona Rawfoot will be after them, you hear me?"

"Oh, I hear ya!" Josh said. "The Lost Plains will be safe in our hands."

Rona went on her way, and together, the rest of them made their way back to the Trihorn Settlement.

Josh suddenly didn't mind that summer was

coming to an end. He'd had a mountain adventure *and* flown on a pterodactyl. He couldn't ask for much more than that!

ABOUT THE AUTHOR

Ever since he was a little boy, Will Dare has been mad about T. rexes and velociraptors. He always wondered what it would be like to live in a world where they were still alive. Now, grown up, he has put pen to paper and imagined just that world. Will lives in rural America with his wife and his best pal, Charge (a dog, not a triceratops).

How to Catch a Dino Thief

Book 4

31901063891131

How to Hog-Tie a T-Rex

Book 3

How to Rope a Giganotosaurus

Book 2

Don't miss the rest of Josh's adventures!

How to Tame a Triceratops

Book 1